# The Best Day Ever

### Music by Tom Kenny & Andy Paley

This animated movie is based on Nickelodeon's TV series which features the adventures of SpongeBob and his various friends in Bikini Bottom, an underwater city. Its creator, Stephen Hillenburg, had his initial ideas whilst teaching and studying marine biology, before leaving to fulfil his dreams of becoming an animator.

**Hints & Tips:** Keep the slurred minims *legato* (smooth). Control the top G (bars 20, 24, 28 and 32), practise it and concentrate on the tuning.

# The Bare Necessities

## Music by Terry Gilkyson

The Sherman Brothers were enlisted to completely rewrite the music for this animated feature, based on the book of the same name by Rudyard Kipling. Composed by long-time Disney collaborator Terry Gilkyson and sung by characters Baloo and Mowgli, this song was the only track to survive from the earlier, rejected draft.

**Hints & Tips:** Although mostly in the clarion register (B on the stave to C above the stave), there are places where the melody of this song dips into the chalumeau register (all notes from B♭ on the stave and below). The high notes need to be practised, but spend time on the break between these two registers, which is difficult and vital for becoming a good clarinettist.

# Beyond The Sea

### Words by Charles Trenet • Music by Charles Trenet & Albert Lasry

'La Mer' was originally a 1946 hit for Charles Trenet and his rendition can be heard in the Steve Martin movie *L.A. Story*. In the early 60s Bobby Darin had a hit with this English lyric version (renamed 'Beyond The Sea') and Robbie Williams reprised it for *Finding Nemo*.

**Hints & Tips:** The key changes twice before reverting to the home key of F major, so practise each section separately before piecing the song together.

# Boogie Wonderland

## Words & Music by Jon Lind & Allee Willis

Unable to sing, misfit penguin Mumble has however an extraordinary talent for tap dancing, through which he eventually discovers that this 1979 disco classic by Earth, Wind & Fire is his heart song. Happy that he and Gloria can now be mates, the pair begin dancing, along with all the other penguins in chilly Antarctica.

**Hints & Tips:** Keep the articulation (the attack of a note, such as *staccato*, *tenuto* etc.) clear and crisp, maintaining a focussed sound.

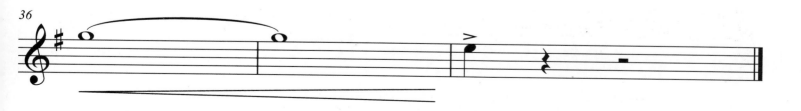

# Can I Have This Dance

## Music by Adam Anders & Nikki Hassman

In this third instalment of Disney's phenomenal success, the students are coming to terms with the reality of going their separate ways after graduation. This song features twice, first as Gabriella teaches Troy the waltz and again as he convinces her to return from university to take part in the school's final musical show.

**Hints & Tips:** When there are a collection of repeated notes in a piece it is stylish to make a small crescendo, or sometimes a diminuendo through them, so at bars 33, 35, 41 and 43, make a small crescendo through the repeated E to add some interest.

# Car Wash

## Words & Music by Norman Whitfield

In 1977, American soul band Rose Royce had a No.1 in the US with this disco hit which Christina Aguilera and Missy Elliott perform on the soundtrack of the 2004 animated comedy *Shark Tale* in which, to advance his own standing in the community, Oscar, a young fish, falsely claims to have killed the son of a shark mob boss.

**Hints & Tips:** Be sure to play all the correct accidentals, these are temporary alterations in pitch, such as sharps (♯), flats (♭) and naturals (♮), those that don't appear in the key signature.

**1.**

**2.**

13

# Copacabana (At The Copa)

**Words & Music by Barry Manilow, Jack Feldman & Bruce Sussman**

In 1978 this song became Barry Manilow's first international hit and earned him his first Grammy Award and a first gold single for a song that he composed. It tells the story of a showgirl, Lola, and her lover Tony, a bartender at the Copacabana, a famous night club in New York City named after a district of Rio de Janeiro.

**Hints & Tips:** Play bars 23–25 in one breath, softly, so the air doesn't escape too fast. Take a good, full breath in preparation.

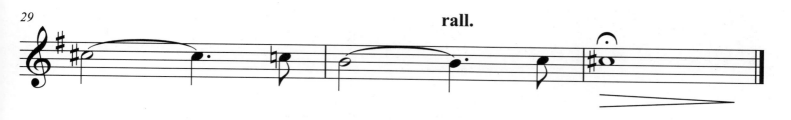

# Food, Glorious Food

## Words & Music by Lionel Bart

This is the opening song from the movie, based on the famous Charles Dickens novel *Oliver Twist*, and is sung by the hungry orphan boys as they fantasise about food while going to collect their dinner from the staff of the workhouse, only to be fed just gruel. Despite this, Oliver gathers up the courage to ask for more!

**Hints & Tips:** The music passes fast in this song and although in $\frac{2}{4}$ (two crotchet beats in a bar), it is easier to think of one in a bar, or concentrate on the first beat of each bar. This will also help you to play the triplets evenly.

16

SHREK

# I'm A Believer

**Words & Music by Neil Diamond**

Awarded the first Oscar for Best Animated Feature, a category introduced in 2001, *Shrek* made notable use of pop music, including this Neil Diamond song which was a 1967 No.1 hit on both sides of the Atlantic for The Monkees. At the end, the whole cast sing it as Shrek and his bride Fiona depart on their honeymoon.

**Hints & Tips:** Bar 34 is marked *ff* (fortissimo), meaning very loud, but this doesn't mean make a nasty sound! Aim for a good, focussed sound, which will naturally be loud.

# Kung Fu Fighting

**Words & Music by Carl Douglas**

In 1974, at the peak of the craze for martial arts, this song was a one-hit wonder for Carl Douglas in both the UK and US. A reworked version was included in the 2008 movie, set in ancient China, in which Po, a lazy, obese panda moves from working in his family's noodle shop to fulfil his aspiration of being a kung fu master.

**Hints & Tips:** The rhythm is often syncopated in this song, which means the weak beats are accented, so work it out slowly before playing with the CD backing track. Practising with a metronome would be useful.

# Oompa Loompa

## Words & Music by Leslie Bricusse & Anthony Newley

In the 1971 film, based on a 1964 Roald Dahl novel, Charlie Bucket is fortunate to be chosen as one of five children allowed to go inside the most popular and powerful chocolate factory in the world which, because of the risk of industrial espionage, is staffed entirely by Oompa Loompa, mischievous dwarfs who love singing.

**Hints & Tips:** Playing the written articulation will bring this song to life; make a distinction between *staccato*, *accents* and non-articulated notes. When a piece is fast it is easy to play too loudly, but this song is mostly marked *mp* (moderately soft), so follow the dynamics.

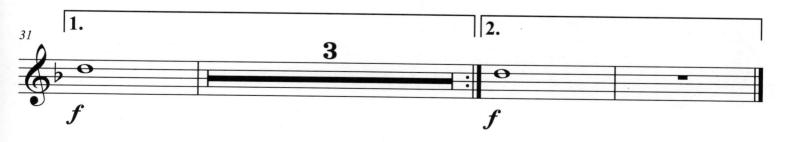

# Ordinary Miracle

**Words & Music by Glen Ballard & Dave Stewart**

This haunting, sentimental song was recorded by Sarah McLachlan for the 2006 film, based on a novel, first published in 1952, by E. B. White in which Wilbur the pig is saved from slaughter by Charlotte, an intelligent barn spider, who writes messages praising him in her web in order to persuade the farmer to let him live.

**Hints & Tips:** Because of the repetitive nature of this song, once you have learned the opening phrase (bars 1–4) you will have a good grasp of the entire song. For the same reason, it could easily sound uninteresting, combat this by following the dynamics (gradations of volume, e.g. *p*, *mp*, *f* etc.) and maybe adding some of your own. Beginning the song quietly would be a good start.

# Somewhere Out There

**Words & Music by James Horner, Barry Mann & Cynthia Weil**

*An American Tail* was the first animated film made by Universal Pictures and features Fievel, a young Russian mouse, separated from his family on the way to America, a land they think is without cats. The song, which won two 1988 Grammy Awards, describes their hope of being able to see each other again.

**Hints & Tips:** This is a pretty melody that should be played gently, as marked. Good breath control is needed for the long phrases in bars 21–29, blowing softly and taking good breaths when possible is the key.

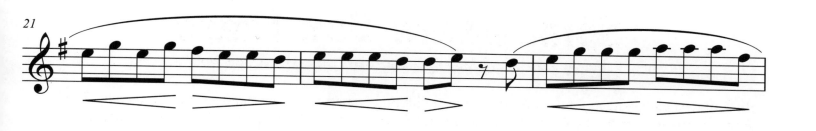

# That's How You Know

**Words by Stephen Schwartz • Music by Alan Menken**

In a film which heralded a return by Disney to traditional animation, this song is performed by Amy Adams as Giselle, an archetypal Disney Princess, as she questions Robert, a handsome lawyer, on his views about love after finding out that he has been with his girlfriend Nancy for five years and has yet to propose to her.

**Hints & Tips:** There are many repeated notes in this song, play them evenly so that each is no more prominent than the next. Beware of the accidentals.

**Moderate Latin feel**

# You've Got A Friend In Me

**Words & Music by Randy Newman**

Since the 1980s, Randy Newman has worked mainly as a film composer, his work on *Toy Story* establishing his trademark animation sound, subsequently carried over to several other scores for Pixar films. Nominated for an Oscar for this song, Newman finally won such an award in 2002 after no fewer than 15 unfruitful nominations.

**Hints & Tips:** Bars 33–34 will require practise with the CD; the *rallentando* (slow down gradually) and *a tempo* (return to original speed) should be accurate, otherwise these bars will be messy.

**Easy shuffle feel**

# Don't Worry, Be Happy

## Words & Music by Bobby McFerrin

Taking its title from a famous quote by the Indian mystic Meher Baba, this became the first *a cappella* song to reach No.1 on the Billboard Hot 100 and won a 1989 Grammy Award for Record Of The Year and Song Of The Year, although composer Bobby McFerrin never received any significant airplay for any other song!

**Hints & Tips:** To get an idea of how reggae sounds, listen to some reggae music, or alternatively, listen to the musicians on the accompanying CD. There are many upbeats (the note(s) preceding a melody, from the previous bar) which need to be neat and rhythmic as it is easy to come in too late, so breathe in good time.

**Moderate Reggae feel (swung ♪'s)**

1 2 3 4 5 6 7 8 9